Princess Poppy
The Big Mix-Up

Princess Poppy
The Big Mix-Up

written by Janey Louise Jones
Illustrated by Samantha Chaffey

THE BIG MIX-UP
A YOUNG CORGI BOOK 978 0 552 55951 5

First published in Great Britain by Young Corgi,
an imprint of Random House Children's Publishers UK

Young Corgi edition published 2007

The Random House Group Limited supports The Forest Stewardship Council
(FSC®), the leading international forest certification organisation. Our books
carrying the FSC label are printed on FSC® certified paper. FSC is the only forest
certification scheme endorsed by the leading environmental organisations, including
Greenpeace. Our paper procurement policy can be found at
www.randomhouse.co.uk/environment

MIX
Paper from
responsible sources
FSC® C016897

Set in 14/21pt Bembo MT Schoolbook by
Falcon Oast Graphic Art Ltd.

Young Corgi Books are published by Random House Children's Publishers UK,
61–63 Uxbridge Road, London W5 5SA

www.randomhousechildrens.co.uk
www.princesspoppy.com

Addresses for companies within The Random House Group Limited can be
found at: www.randomhouse.co.uk/offices.htm

THE RANDOM HOUSE GROUP Limited Reg. No. 954009

A CIP catalogue record for this book is available from the British Library.

Printed and bound by CPI Group (UK) Ltd,
Croydon, CR0 4YY

*For gossiping girls
everywhere: beware!*

Chapter One

Ever since Poppy's twin brother and sister,
Angel and Archie, were born earlier that
summer, Poppy's cousin Saffron had been
over at Honeysuckle Cottage even more
often than usual. Saffron was much older
than Poppy, but they were very close. Poppy
had been her bridesmaid when Saffron
married the village vet, David Sage.

Saffron absolutely adored the twins and
spent hours cooing over them. So one day it
was decided that Poppy, Mum and Saffron

would do a swap. Saffron would come and
look after the twins for the day while Poppy
and Mum went to work in her shop.
Poppy was thrilled: she had always wanted
to work in the shop because it was so
glamorous – plus it would be nice to have
Mum all to herself for the day!

"I can't wait to be in charge of Saffron's
shop!" Poppy said to herself as she started to
get ready for her big day at work. *What
would a fashion designer wear?* she wondered as
she surveyed all the
clothes in her wardrobe.

Poppy began to try
on outfits, admiring
herself in her long
mirror each time she put
on something different.

"Too party-girl," she
said as she threw a
sparkly dress across her

2

bed. "Too pony-girl," she decided as she discarded a jeans and wellies combo. Shorts and a T-shirt were "too sporty-girl". She eventually settled on a pretty red skirt and cute white top, with red ankle-strap sandals and a silver sequinned bag. She gathered together everything she thought she might need for the day and put it in her bag: a notebook, coloured pencils, perfume and a hairbrush – it was vital to look good at the shop!

"I'm ready," Poppy called as she raced down the stairs. "Wow! You look *lovely*, Mum!" she said admiringly. Poppy hadn't liked to mention it, but since the twins were born Mum had been looking a bit scruffy.

But today she was wearing a pretty yellow dress with a wide belt and matching kitten-heeled shoes. Plus she had put on pearl earrings *and* make-up!

"Thank you, darling," smiled Mum. "And you look lovely too."

Just as Mum was wondering where Saffron had got to, she saw her niece walking up the garden path and waving at them cheerily. Poppy rushed to the window to see what her cousin was wearing – Saffron had such a great eye for fashion. But Poppy was rather disappointed by what she

saw. Saffron looked perfectly nice, but what surprised Poppy was that she looked very . . . well, ordinary and sensible. For Saffron this was definitely extraordinary! She was wearing some old jeans with a loose emerald-green kaftan top and flat gold gladiator sandals. Her beautiful red hair was tied back in a ponytail and she wasn't even wearing any make-up.

"I'm dressed for childcare!" Saffron explained as she saw the look on Poppy's face, which seemed to say, *Why don't you look as glamorous as usual?* "I've cut my nails short so that I don't scratch the babies, and I've taken off all my jewellery except my wedding and engagement rings."

"That's very sensible, Saffron," replied Mum. "Angel absolutely loves all things sparkly and shiny – she'd be tugging at your earrings and beads in no time if you hadn't taken them off."

Saffron smiled. She was so excited about looking after the babies, but even though she had spent a lot of time with them since they were born, she was a little nervous – her aunt had always been there, just in case.

"Let's sit down and have a cup of tea and I'll go through everything with you," suggested Mum.

"Thanks, Aunt Lavender," replied Saffron. "I really hope I can manage everything."

"Don't worry, you'll be just fine. Poppy and I have made a list for you so you don't forget anything. Even if you do, you can always give me a ring at the shop," reassured Mum as she unfolded a large piece of paper with writing all over it.

Angel and Archie's Day

9 a.m.: Milk feeds. Mix baby rice with 2oz milk. Spoon feed. <u>Don't forget bibs!</u>
Change nappies after breakfast and get the twins dressed.
Classical music baby CDs calm them down if they're misbehaving!

10 a.m.: Take for a short walk in pram. <u>Don't forget to take rattles, bottles of sterilized water and spare nappies and wipes</u> just in case.

10.30 a.m.: Put the twins down for a nap — they usually sleep for about an hour.

While they're sleeping, please put a wash on & hang up wet clothes in garden. Prepare lunch (pureed carrots, sweet potatoes and apples).

12 p.m.: Lunch, includes milk feed. <u>Don't forget bibs!</u>

1 p.m.: Nappies will probably need changing and clothes as well (will be messy from lunch). Put another wash on.

1.30 p.m.: Walk to shop for fruit and vegetables, baby rice and baby bubble bath — the General Store has my order, it just needs collecting.

3 p.m.: Put them down for another nap. Bring in dry washing and hang out wet. Make a start on casserole for supper—ingredients in cupboard and fridge and recipe on fridge. There are lots of toys and a play mat for when twins wake up.

4 p.m.: Prepare the twins' tea and feed them by 5 p.m. (milk feed and porridge).

5.30 p.m.: <u>Bath time</u>. Fill baby baths with bubbles and warm (not hot) water, warm towels on towel rail.

6.30 p.m.: <u>Bed time</u>. Put on new nappies and clean pyjamas and tuck them into their cots. Read a story or sing a lullaby.

Saffron read through
the list and gasped.

"When will I have
my meals and read
my *Buttons and
Bows* magazine?"
she asked.

Mum laughed. "Try
to squeeze your snacks and reading times in
during their naps or you'll never eat or
relax!" she explained.

"Those babies are really hard work, you
know," exclaimed Poppy as she put on her
new hat – she didn't really need it, but it
went so well with her outfit.

"Yes, I'm just beginning to realize how
much!" said Saffron. "Here's the key for the
shop. Now, off you go! I'm expecting a
delivery of silver buttons at nine – Charlie
will be dropping them off! I've left
instructions for you in the shop to help you

through the day," she went on as Mum and Poppy kissed the twins goodbye and wished her luck. "Ring me if you need anything," she called after them, suddenly starting to worry that Mum and Poppy might not manage.

Mum took a deep breath. Surely running the shop would be easier than a whole day with the twins.

Chapter Two

The delivery van, with Charlie at the wheel,
was waiting when Poppy and Mum arrived
at the shop. They were both a bit breathless
because they'd run there so as not to miss
him. Poor Mum could hardly manage in
her kitten heels.

"Oh, I haven't worn these shoes for years.
They're agony!" she complained.

Mum opened up the shop with the key
Saffron had given her and waved to Charlie
to come in. Saffron had left sticky notes all

over the place, so while Mum dealt with the delivery Poppy looked at them all – she was eager to start work and desperate to do a good job.

"Where's Saffron today?" asked Charlie.

"Oh, well, we've done a swap! She's looking after my babies while my daughter and I look after her shop. Just for today," explained Mum.

"I see. That's a shame – I had a tasty little titbit of gossip for her," said Charlie.

"Is it something you can tell me?" asked Mum. "I'm Saffron's Aunt Lavender – I'd be happy to give her a message."

"Thanks very much – as long as you can keep a secret. Y'see, what it is . . ." At that point he dropped his voice to a whisper so Poppy couldn't hear exactly what he was saying. "See, I've just been at Bijou in Camomile Cove," he continued, "and Gabriella, the manageress, was saying that there's a strange lady visiting all the clothes shops round this way at the moment, taking notes and nosing about. She asks lots of questions too, but never buys anything. Gabriella reckons she's planning to open her own shop and she's stealing ideas from all the competition. So, when you think about it, Lavender – you don't mind if I call you that, do you? – she's nothing more than a thief."

Although this wasn't good news, it was obvious that Charlie was enjoying being the bringer of what he thought was top-secret information.

Mum nodded silently. "Right-o, Charlie. I'll let Saffron know," she replied, even though she was sure there was no truth in Charlie's gossip. "Thanks for telling me. We'll keep an eye out as well. Bye!"

Oh no! A thief in Honeypot Hill, thought Poppy, not fully understanding what Charlie

14

had meant. *That's terrible! I'll make sure she doesn't steal anything from this shop while I'm in charge!*

When Charlie had left, Mum made a note of his message and looked around the shop. She was always very proud to see some of the hats she had made displayed by Saffron alongside matching dresses, shoes and bags. Sometimes they even designed ranges together. Meanwhile Poppy carried on with her tour of the shop, reading Saffron's notes as she went along. There was a note on the till:

Float should
stay same
all day –
£30.

"What's the float?" asked Poppy.

"It's money in the till in case the first few customers need change," explained Mum.

Next, they looked at the antique tailor's dummy that Saffron used when she was making clothes. It was draped with strings of creamy pearls and adorned with a huge dusky pink rose. There was a note on that too:

To take an order, please write down all measurements and note which fabric & design is required. Take the customer's full name and address and the date they need the item to be ready.

There were also notes on the telephone, in the window and about ten more on the gorgeous glass-fronted wooden drawers filled with buttons, zips, sequins and bows. Even the dresses hanging on the "for collection" rail had notes on them. It was the village party that weekend so Saffron had been busy making beautiful new outfits for lots of the women in the village.

"D'you think Saffron's worried we'll get all muddled up, Mum?" asked Poppy.

Mum laughed. "Maybe, but it's only natural. We left *her* quite a lot of instructions too!"

"Yeah, I suppose so, but I think looking after the shop's going to be easy-peasy lemon-squeezy! Much easier than looking after Angel and Archie," replied Poppy.

"Oh, Poppy, don't be so sure. Anyway, I'm sure Saffron'll do a great job," said Mum, biting her lip. She really wanted the swap to work: it would be great to be able to do it again. It was lovely to be spending a whole day with Poppy – it was very important to show her that she was still her little princess even though she had the twins as well now. Poppy was finding it hard to get used to sharing her mum and dad.

While Mum busied herself with unpacking the delivery, Poppy decided to go and

explore the parts of the shop that she didn't usually go into, like the workshop in the basement. She headed down the rickety wooden stairs to explore the heart of Saffron's fashion business. The place where the ideas became reality! It was so exciting.

A beautiful pendant light with amber-coloured glass droplets dangling from a faded bronze candelabra hung from the ceiling.

"Wow!" exclaimed Poppy as she turned to look at the rolls of jewel-coloured fabrics and rows of silky threads and bobbins. There were two more tailor's dummies, decorated again with pearls and silk flowers, each wearing partially made ball gowns. One dress was a deep peacock-blue and the other a soft shell-pink. The whole scene was magical. It made Poppy think of dances at Cornsilk Castle and midnight balls, just like in *Cinderella*. The walls were covered with Saffron's designs. She had dreamed up whole ranges of clothes and accessories – all of which Poppy would have loved to have for herself. Poppy looked with wonder at the designs.

lavender

Fragrant lavender ball gowns, inspired by the soothing Lavender Garden where I spent much of my childhood

Barley necklaces inspired by harvest on Barley Farm.

Fairy dresses with spring cherry-blossom wings.

Wow! thought Poppy. *Saffron's designs are all based on the places I know. Maybe that's why I like her fashions so much!*

Dressing-up clothes:

bumblebees and butterflies, ladybirds and spiders

A honeysuckle party dress for a special occasion and a pale golden wedding dress to be worn at Cornsilk Castle when a fairytale princess marries her knight in shining armour

Then she noticed a sweet little wooden wardrobe. It was painted pale blue and the doors were decorated with painted flowers.

"I wish I had something like that in my bedroom," she said to herself. All Saffron's things were so gorgeous.

Next, Poppy's eye was caught by some small colourful garments hanging on a rail in the corner.

"Children's clothes. Yippee!" she cried.

Poppy looked at the row of party dresses in all sizes from teeny-tiny baby up to . . . well, Poppy's own size and beyond. Her eye was particularly drawn to a floaty lilac dress with a label that read:

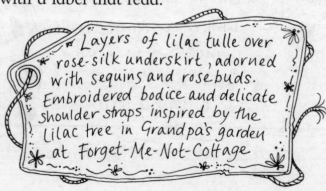

Layers of lilac tulle over rose-silk underskirt, adorned with sequins and rose-buds. Embroidered bodice and delicate shoulder straps inspired by the lilac tree in Grandpa's garden at Forget-Me-Not-Cottage

That would be perfect for me, thought Poppy. *A dress dreamed up from my grandpa's garden.*

She danced around the workshop with the dress, humming *I Could Have Danced All Night* to herself. (Poppy's absolute favourite musical was *My Fair Lady*.) But just at that moment she heard the bell ring in the shop above her. Their first customer of the day must have arrived! What Poppy really wanted to do was try the dress on. Then she remembered how much trouble she had caused when she had tried on Saffron's wedding dress without asking just hours before the wedding, so she resisted temptation and ran upstairs to help Mum.

You never know, it might be that nasty thief Charlie was talking about! thought Poppy, quite excited at the prospect of a little drama.

Chapter Three

Their first customer of the day was Madame
Angelwing, Poppy's ballet teacher. She had
all her clothes made at Saffron's Sewing
Shop and had done so ever since the shop
opened. She always looked terribly stylish.

"Good morning! What can we do for
you today, Madame Angelwing?" asked
Mum.

"Oh, do call me Eloise," said Madame
graciously. "I'm here to pick up my new
dress for the village party. I'll need to try it

on to check it fits properly too. Where's Saffron?"

"Saffron's minding Angel and Archie for the day and Poppy and I are running the shop," explained Mum. Although she looked and sounded calm, Mum was actually rather flustered. There was so much to do and she hadn't yet had time to read all Saffron's notes or check the diary for the day's appointments. Saffron had always made running the shop seem so easy.

While Mum went to have a look for Madame Angelwing's dress on the "for collection" rail, Madame looked around the shop.

"I notice the display is the same as last week," she observed sniffily. "Saffron always changes her window display every week."

"Oh, dear, does she?" said Mum, all a-fluster.

"I could change it, Mum," suggested Poppy excitedly.

25

Mum turned round and nodded cautiously. "OK, darling. That would be great."

Poppy went outside to have a good look at the existing window display – she wanted the new one to be completely different and amazing! As she did so, she glanced back into the shop, and at that moment, a small gust of wind blew the changing-room curtain up for just a second or two and revealed Mum helping Madame Angelwing into her new dress. Poppy couldn't believe what she had seen – her stylish and elegant Parisian ballet teacher was wearing huge bloomers that came right down to her knees and a very old-fashioned corset!

"I must tell Honey about Madame's underwear," Poppy giggled to herself. "She'll think it's hilarious!"

When she'd stopped laughing at the thought of Madame Angelwing's funny undies, Poppy carried on looking at the

window and trying to decide what she should do for the new display, half listening to Mum and Madame Angelwing chatting away in the changing room at the same time.

"When are you expecting the results from the ballet exam, Madame, er, Eloise?" asked Mum. "Poppy has been absolutely desperate to know ever since she took the exam. She worked so hard for it, as did all the other girls."

"Ah! The subject on all our minds," replied Madame Angelwing. "The exam results came through today—"

At the mention of the ballet exam Poppy's ears pricked up and she strained to hear exactly what was being said, which was quite tricky from where she was standing outside the shop. She had butterflies in her tummy wondering how she had done. What if she hadn't passed? What if Honey had done better than she had? Poppy decided to go back inside and pretend she was looking for some things for the window display so that she could hear better. Mum was concentrating so hard on looking after Madame Angelwing that she didn't notice Poppy come back in. Poppy busied herself choosing scarves and bracelets to include in her display, trying very hard to listen in on Mum and Madame's conversation!

"What a fright I had this morning!"
Madame continued. "At first I thought that
Honey, Mimosa, Abigail and Sweetpea had
all failed!"

But just then, a new customer arrived and
since Mum was busy, Poppy had to serve
her. It was a very pretty young woman of
about Saffron's age. She smiled at Poppy and
Poppy smiled back timidly, still trying to
listen to Madame but also wondering if this
new customer was the thief Charlie had
warned Mum about earlier. The lady
looked all around the shop and
asked Poppy lots of questions
about designs and
fabrics and
accessories and how
long it would take
to have a dress
made for her.
Poppy answered

the questions as well as she could and the
lady seemed satisfied. Poppy was enjoying
herself playing the shopkeeper, but it did
mean that she could only hear the odd
snippet of Mum and Madame Angelwing's
conversation.

While Poppy looked after the customer,
Madame Angelwing continued to explain
to Mum what had happened that morning
with the ballet results and why she thought
everyone had failed.

"The Royal Ballet board has re-designed
the certificates and all the colours have
changed. A red is now a fail, while a purple
is a pass. It used to be the exact opposite.
But then I realized that everyone had passed!
So, imagine it, Lavender! At first I thought
my girls had all failed! But not so – they
have done very well indeed. And Poppy too:
she alone has passed with distinction," she
concluded.

Unfortunately what Poppy heard, in between chatting to the new customer and eavesdropping on Mum and her ballet teacher was: ". . . Honey, Mimosa, Abigail and Sweetpea . . . all failed . . . And Poppy . . . has passed with distinction."

Poppy couldn't believe her ears. She knew all her friends were good dancers. This was terrible news, although she *was* thrilled that she had passed — and with distinction!

Chapter Four

The suspicious customer carried on browsing
and Poppy went back to working on her
window display, keeping an eye on the lady
all the while. She was looking at a particular
necklace for ages and writing something
down in a little notebook too. Poppy thought
this was rather odd, but before she had a
chance to say anything, Madame and Mum
came out of the changing room.

"Just wrap up the dress, Lavender,"
Madame Angelwing said to Mum. "I'll take

it away today. I *am* looking forward to wearing it."

Then she turned to Poppy. "Have you decided what theme you will have in your window, Poppy?"

"Well," she replied, "since everyone calls me Princess Poppy, I have chosen 'princesses' as my theme."

"Hah! I should have known. What a good choice. Good luck with it," said the ballet teacher as she swept out of the shop with her new dress beautifully wrapped in pale-green tissue paper and rose-pink ribbon, all popped inside one of Saffron's gorgeous boutique bags.

"Mum, I need to talk to you," whispered Poppy after Madame Angelwing had left. "I think that lady over there is the thief the delivery man was talking about."

"Sssshhh, Poppy," said Mum sharply, worried that the customer would hear. "She doesn't look like a thief to me. Anyway, you shouldn't listen to gossip.

"Can I help you?" she asked the lady.

"Oh, yes please. I've been invited to a big wedding and I need a new dress and possibly one of these lovely matching hats. May I try on some outfits now that the changing room is free?" she asked.

"Of course, come this way," replied Mum as she led the customer to the changing room.

The lady tried on several dresses, then looked at Saffron's dress designs for that season. Mum took her

measurements, just like Saffron had
explained in her note. Although she really
wanted to make a sale, Mum was keen to
get this customer out of the shop before
Poppy repeated any more village gossip and
lost Saffron a customer for good, so she
worked quickly!

"Would you like to go ahead with the
order?" asked Mum.

"I'm not quite sure yet," the lady replied.

"There's a dress that I really like in another shop and I just can't decide between them. I'll come back later. Thank you so much for your help."

Although this seemed perfectly normal to Mum – she'd often been indecisive about such things herself – she could see from Poppy's face that *she* thought this was very suspicious behaviour indeed.

"Don't say a word, darling," Mum said to Poppy after the lady had left. "She was going to a wedding – there's nothing strange in that, there are always lots of weddings in the summer. We don't even know that there is a thief – Charlie was just gossiping. You shouldn't believe everything you hear!"

Poppy still firmly believed that there was a thief in the village, whatever Mum thought. But she also knew that Mum wanted to hear no more about it so she decided to change the subject.

"Mum, I need to get a few princess things from home to finish my window display. Can I go now?" she asked. "I won't be long."

"OK then, but let's have our break first," decided Mum, who was rather exhausted by the exacting ballet teacher and all the other goings-on. "I'll have a coffee and you can have a strawberry shake and we can both have one of the iced cakes Granny Bumble made."

Poppy nodded, flipped the sign on the shop door round to CLOSED and then settled down for her break.

Chapter Five

Refreshed after her mid-morning break,
Poppy skipped the short distance home,
thinking about which dolls, tiaras, jewels,
feather boas and other princess things she
would need for the window. But all that was
forgotten when she walked into the cottage
– it was complete pandemonium!

"Oh, Poppy, I'm *so* glad to see you!" said
Saffron as she looked up and noticed her
younger cousin.

Poor Saffron was in such a state that she

didn't even think to ask why Poppy had come home.

"I'm a bit worked up, I'm afraid. I'm just no good at this. While I was giving Angel her milk, Archie was screaming. So I put Angel down in the pram 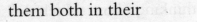 and picked up Archie, but then Angel started screaming. So I propped them both up on the sofa with cushions and fed them both at once! Then the doorbell rang, so I had to put 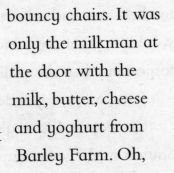 them both in their bouncy chairs. It was only the milkman at the door with the milk, butter, cheese and yoghurt from Barley Farm. Oh, that reminds me – they're not in the fridge yet. Then I burned the vegetables I was

cooking for their lunch. Anyway, next thing
I knew, they both needed changing. We
haven't even been out yet and I am way
behind with Aunt Lavender's list of things
to do. Could you look after them for ten
or fifteen minutes while I put everything in
the fridge and have a cup of coffee? If I
was at the shop I would have had my
mid-morning break by now. I'm just feeling
so frazzled – I'm completely exhausted,"
said Saffron as she poured out her troubles.

Poppy had never seen Saffron like this before. But then she remembered how hard she had found it when the twins were born and how she'd worn earmuffs to shut out their crying and even run away to her tree house to escape them.

"I just need to get some princess stuff from my room for the new window display at the shop and then I'll look after the twins while you take a break," replied Poppy.

"Oh, thank you, Poppy. I was going to do the window yesterday but then I decided that it would be a fun job for you – something you'd be really good at it – so I thought I'd leave it," replied Saffron. She seemed much happier now that she knew she was going to have time to sit down with her *Buttons and Bows* magazine and a cup of coffee.

When Poppy had gathered together everything she needed, she went back

downstairs to play with Angel and Archie
so that Saffron could take her break.
She put on a little puppet show for them
with her princess dolls: the twins screamed
with delight as she invented voices for each
doll and acted out a squabble between the

princesses. Twenty minutes later Saffron came in from the garden looking refreshed and ready to take over again.

"Thank you, Poppy. You've saved my life!" she said as she adjusted her ponytail and put on some pretty pink lipstick. Poppy smiled proudly, put her princess backpack over her shoulders and said goodbye to her cousin and her little brother and sister.

"Oh, Saffron," said Poppy as she walked out of the back door, "I forgot to say – Charlie left a message for you. He said to

44

tell you that there's a thief in the area. He
told us to look out for her."

"Right, Poppy, thanks for telling me. Let
me know if you see anything suspicious
today," replied Saffron, thinking what a
terrible gossip Charlie was.

Chapter Six

On the way back to the shop Poppy bumped into her best friend, Honey.

"Hello, Princess Poppy! What are you up to?" asked Honey.

"I'm working in Saffron's Sewing Shop with Mum today and Saffron's looking after Angel and Archie," explained Poppy. "I've just been home to get some of my princess things for the new window display."

"Wow, that sounds like loads of fun," smiled Honey.

"The cottage is a total mess though. Saffron's finding the twins really difficult to cope with so I looked after them while she had a break and she said that I totally saved her life!" boasted Poppy. "I'm just going back to the shop now actually. It's so great working there. The clothes are so pretty, plus I get to hear about everything that's going on in the village."

"That's amazing," Honey replied. "Have you heard anything interesting today?"

"Yeah – Charlie, the delivery man, told us that there's a thief operating in the village, so I've been looking out for her all day," she replied.

Honey looked very impressed.

"And I know what Madame Angelwing wears under her clothes," Poppy giggled.

"How?" asked Honey, wide-eyed in disbelief.

"Well, she was trying on her dress for the

47

village party, and the curtain blew open a tiny bit, so I could see in. Guess what she was wearing?"

"Her clothes are always beautiful so I'm sure her underwear is too. I bet she wears silk French knickers and a matching camisole," Honey replied confidently.

"Wrong," grinned Poppy triumphantly. "Madame wears giant polka-dot knickers all the way to her knees and a huge corset too!"

While Poppy and Honey were laughing about Madame's bloomers, Mimosa appeared from the direction of the Hedgerows Hotel.

"What's all this about Madame's big pants?" she asked.

Poppy told the story all over again and the three of them collapsed in a heap of giggles. *Knowing all the village gossip before her friends was the best!* Poppy thought to herself.

"I'd better get back to the shop now. I told Mum I wouldn't be long," she said as she turned to leave her two friends. Just then she remembered that she had some other news and she knew Honey and Mimosa would both want to hear it. "Oh, and actually, I heard something else too. I'm afraid it's not good news though," she added, trying to sound sympathetic. "Quite a few girls have failed the ballet exam!"

"How do you know that?" asked Honey.

"Madame Angelwing told us," Poppy answered confidently, even though this wasn't exactly how it had happened.

"Do you know who's failed?" Honey asked nervously.

"Well, that's why it's not good news. You two, Sweetpea and Abigail have all failed, I'm afraid," said Poppy, sounding a little too perky for the bringer of such bad news.

Both girls burst into tears. "But I did so much practice," Honey sobbed. "*And*

Madame Angelwing said I was the best ballerina in her class when she picked me to play Coppelia."

"I practised really hard as well," said Mimosa quietly. "I don't understand how we could have failed."

Poppy remembered about Coppelia only too well. She had been devastated when Honey was chosen for the main part. They had even fallen out over it briefly. In fact, now that she thought about it properly, it *did* seem very unlikely that all the other girls in her ballet class had failed the exam.

Poppy felt very bad indeed. "Whoops, maybe I shouldn't have told you." She felt more guilty than ever. What if she hadn't heard correctly? "I've really got to go now," she told her friends. "*Byee!*"

Poppy had a knot in her tummy as she walked towards the shop. She realized that she had got carried away and said too much. She tried to push it to the back of her mind and hoped that everyone else would just forget too.

Chapter Seven

"Hi, Mum!" said Poppy as she walked into
the shop. "Has anything exciting happened
while I was at home?"

"Hello, Poppy. Well, I seem to have
everything under control at last. I've read all
Saffron's notes, done a stock-take of ribbon
and placed the order with All Tied Up. I've
also cleared a bit more of the window out
for you so you can get started on the new
display. Oh, and I've sold a dress to Natasha
Melody," said Mum. "It seems as if almost

everyone in the village is buying a new outfit for the party. Maybe I should get one too.

"Wow, it's been really busy," said Poppy as she unpacked the things she'd collected from home. "I don't think I'll be leaving the shop again today – there's way too much exciting stuff happening here."

"How's Saffron getting on with the babies?" asked Mum, as casually as possible.

"Well," sighed Poppy, "not so well, actually. The house is a huge mess: there's stuff everywhere. I'd say that it's even worse than when Dad is in charge. The twins were both crying, probably because they were hungry, the washing was still in the wash basket and Saffron hadn't prepared their lunch yet. She was totally stressed and the twins weren't even dressed! It was a *disaster*! Saffron is much better at looking after the shop than she is at looking after babies," concluded Poppy with a dramatic flourish.

What Poppy didn't say was that by the time she'd left, everything was back to normal and Saffron was completely in control of the situation, if a little behind with Mum's list of things to do.

"Oh dear, poor Saffron. It's all my fault. I should have known it was too soon to leave her to look after the babies on her own. I've got so used to the routine now, it doesn't seem so daunting. I should have done a day  with her and the twins before we did the swap. What am I going to do?" said Mum.

Just then the shop bell chimed, announcing

55

the arrival of another customer. This time it
was Poppy's teacher, Holly Mallow.

"Hello, Lavender! Hello, Poppy!" said
Miss Mallow cheerfully. "What a nice
surprise to see you two in here."

"Oh, Holly! How nice to see you too,"
replied Mum.

"Lavender, are you feeling all right?"
asked Miss Mallow. "You're as pale as a
ghost."

"I'm fine, thanks, just missing my twins,"

said Mum, although she didn't sound fine at all. "Poppy and I are looking after the shop today while Saffron looks after them. In fact, do you have time to stay here with Poppy for half an hour or so while I pop home? I just want to check that everything is OK."

"It would be my pleasure, Lavender. Although I'm sure everything is absolutely fine. Saff's a natural with babies," replied Miss Mallow reassuringly.

"Thank you so much. I won't be long," replied Mum, feeling very relieved that she was able to nip home, but also slightly guilty: after what Poppy had told her, she doubted her niece's ability to look after the twins properly.

"Poppy," called Mum as she was

walking out of the door, "when you've finished dressing the window, there's another fun job for you. Saffron is planning to launch a range of children's clothes called the Fairy Garden and she thought you might be able to come up with some ideas for her. She's left a pad and some coloured pencils out for you."

Wow! I'm so lucky, thought Poppy. *I know just what the Fairy Garden collection should look like – all soft petals and sunlight. I can't wait to start sketching. But first I must finish the window display.*

"Come on then," said Miss Mallow. "Show me how you want this window to look. I'll help you put it together."

"I think it should look like a fairytale princess's world. We could peep at her beautiful clothes inside her wardrobe. There's a little empty one in the workshop that we could use. I think we should also have tiaras and sparkly jewellery draped around a pretty mirror. And princess dolls and fairy wands of course," concluded Poppy.

"That sounds wonderful. Let's finish clearing out the old display so we can get on with the new one," said Miss Mallow.

When the window was completely clear, Poppy and Miss Mallow lifted the wardrobe into position. It looked absolutely perfect. In the open wardrobe, on satin-covered coat-hangers, Poppy carefully hung some of the gorgeous little party dresses she'd found in the workshop. Then she draped scarves, fluffy tulle petticoats and a feather boa over the wardrobe doors and laid tiny silk shoes on the floor in front of it. Every so often either Poppy or Miss Mallow would run outside and give a thumbs-up, or say, "Right a bit," or "Left a bit."

"Let's do the jewellery now!" said Miss Mallow, who was really enjoying herself. Next to the wardrobe they positioned a little table covered with a pretty white lace scarf and a mirror to make it look like a dressing table. Next they decorated the mirror with shimmering beads, sparkling tiaras and shining bracelets. Then they ran outside to see how it looked.

"Magnificent," said Miss Mallow. "Saffron will be delighted."

"Now for the finishing touches," said Poppy. "You stay out here."

She ran inside and laid some fine netting from the workshop along the front of the window and placed her princess dolls, several beautifully illustrated fairy story books, some butterfly hairclips and a diamanté brooch along the netting.

"It's just like looking into a dream," called Miss Mallow from outside. "I know I would stop and look at this and then probably come into the shop, which is the whole point of a shop window, isn't it?" She hugged Poppy. "What a clever girl you are. I've had such fun, and to think, I only dropped by for a new scarf!"

Poppy felt so proud and happy that she had almost forgotten how uneasy she felt about what she'd told Honey and Mimosa earlier. But not quite. Whenever she stopped what she was doing, she felt a pang of guilt. So she decided to keep her mind off it by getting started on some sketches for the Fairy Garden.

First she sketched a gorgeous little sun dress. Then a cute red poppy-petal bikini with green straps, then a pair of multi-coloured flowery wellies, a padded jacket for horse-riding, a pink tulle ballet outfit, and

lots of petal party dresses. As well as this, she
drew dressing-up clothes for princess plays,
and pieces of flower jewellery.

Poppy proudly showed her ideas to Miss
Mallow, who was having a coffee in between
serving customers. "And look, this is a
jewelled ballerina tiara," she explained.

"That's lovely," said Miss Mallow. "Oh, in fact, that reminds me: I bumped into Madame Angelwing on the way here and she told me that everyone has passed the ballet exam! Isn't that absolutely marvellous news!"

Poppy suddenly felt all hot and prickly. That wasn't what she'd heard and it certainly wasn't what she'd told Honey and Mimosa. What a mess! How could she have got it so wrong? And what was she going to do now?

"Let's close the shop for a bit and have some lunch in the garden," suggested Miss Mallow, not noticing Poppy's red face and downcast expression. "I'm famished and I think we both deserve a break."

Poppy pushed her worries to the back of her mind as she shut the shop door, turned the sign round to CLOSED and helped Miss Mallow set up the garden table with food

and glasses of cloudy lemonade. Before
long, she was chatting away merrily to
her teacher. She told Miss Mallow what
she'd been up to during the school holidays
and how much she was enjoying working

in the shop. She even passed on all the gossip she'd heard that day, from Charlie's tip-off about the thief to Madame's great big bloomers, Saffron's trouble with the twins and who was buying a new dress for the village party. But she couldn't get what she'd told Honey and Mimosa out of her mind. Suddenly she became very quiet.

"What's the matter?" asked Miss Mallow.

"Um, er, well, the thing is, Miss Mallow, I think I've made a really bad mistake," Poppy blurted out. Then she told her teacher the whole sorry story.

"Oh dear," said Miss Mallow sympathetically. "You *are* in a pickle. We need to sort this out right away before it gets any worse. The best thing to do is admit your mistake and just tell the truth. I'm sure Mimosa and Honey will understand."

Chapter Eight

Meanwhile back at Honeysuckle Cottage
Mum had just arrived to find out what was
happening with Saffron and the twins.

"Hello! Only me," she called as she pushed
open the front door.

"Hi, Aunt Lavender. We're in the kitchen
having lunch," called Saffron. "Come
through."

Mum was slightly nervous about what she
might see when she got to the kitchen but
Saffron's cheery tone eased her mind slightly.

Perhaps Poppy had been exaggerating.

When Mum walked into the kitchen, she saw the twins sitting up nicely in their highchairs, neatly dressed in clean clothes and wearing their bibs. Saffron was expertly feeding them with home-made puréed vegetables, and was even managing to nibble on her own lunch at the same time. She looked very relaxed and so did Angel and Archie.

"Oh," said Mum, surprised and relieved that Saffron was coping so well. "You're managing wonderfully."

"Well, I haven't had time to do everything on your list but I'm doing OK," Saffron replied. "It's actually quite easy once you get into it. I'm having a great time – we should do this again."

Mum felt very silly. From Poppy's description it had sounded as if Saffron was in complete chaos. But the house was spotlessly tidy, Saffron was looking more glamorous than when she'd arrived that morning and the babies were gurgling and laughing.

"Why've you popped home? Did you forget something?" asked Saffron.

"Um, yes. My, um, comfortable shoes! I'll only be a minute," Mum replied. She didn't have the heart to tell her niece that she had doubted her childcare abilities.

"How's the shop?" asked Saffron as Mum appeared with her flat shoes. "Poppy gave me Charlie's message."

"Oh, super. Great. No problems – and it wasn't exactly a message from Charlie, it was just some gossip that he'd picked up. I wouldn't worry about it if I were you. Honestly, Poppy really shouldn't have repeated that – he wasn't even talking to her!" said Mum, slightly annoyed that Poppy had burdened Saffron with any more worries. "In fact, I'd better get back there now. Holly is looking after Poppy for me at the moment and I'm sure she's got things she needs to do."

"She would have called if she was in a hurry," said Saffron. "Why don't you stay and have some lunch? I've made far too much for just me."

"That would be lovely," said Mum as she settled down at the kitchen table and helped herself to some of the yummy-looking salad Saffron had made.

After lunch Mum picked up her sensible shoes, kissed the twins goodbye and left for the shop. She was rather sad that they didn't cry for her to stay, and as she walked along she started to feel rather grumpy. Maybe it was because part of her had hoped that Saffron *was* finding things difficult, especially since it had taken her a while to get into the swing of things when the twins were first born. But it was also because she simply couldn't understand why Poppy had made up all that nonsense about Saffron not coping. She might have been gossiping about what Charlie had said, but it really was very unlike her to make things up.

Chapter Nine

Back at the shop Poppy was sobbing her heart out to her teacher.

"I wasn't lying about the exam results, Miss Mallow. I *did* hear it. Or I *thought* I did. I heard Mum and Madame Angelwing talking and then a customer came in, and because I was serving her I couldn't hear them so well any more," confessed Poppy. "Maybe a tiny little mean part of me only cared that I had passed. I feel so bad about it now."

As Miss Mallow was comforting Poppy, Mum walked through the garden gate looking rather cross. Then she saw that Poppy was upset and all her anger melted away.

"What's wrong, darling?" she asked softly.

Poppy didn't know where to start, and much to her relief, Miss Mallow explained the situation and the muddle that Poppy had got herself into.

"Oh, Poppy! What *has* come over you?" sighed Mum. "It seems you've been gossiping rather a lot today. I just don't understand why you told me that Saffron wasn't coping.

She's doing perfectly well. When I got there, the twins were having lunch; they weren't crying, the washing machine was on and Saffron had even made herself lunch. I couldn't bring myself to tell her that I was checking up on her. I felt terrible, especially when she was managing so well. As for you eavesdropping on my conversation with Madame Angelwing, I am just so disappointed in you. You should know better."

"Lavender, look at the time!" said Miss Mallow, swiftly changing the subject because she could see that Poppy was about to start sobbing again. "We'd better open up the shop – lunch break is over. Oh, and I must have a look at the scarves you've got in stock – that is what I came in for after all!"

So the three of them went back into the shop, unlocked the door and flipped the sign to OPEN.

Poor Poppy felt awful – guilty and confused. Saffron *had* been having a terrible time, although maybe Poppy had exaggerated a bit and she probably shouldn't have told tales. She hung her head. Usually she explained herself and chattered on when she was in trouble, but she felt such a sharp pain of unfairness that she stood completely still and quiet.

"So what are we going to do about the ballet situation?" began Mum, but she was interrupted by the chiming of the doorbell and the arrival of more customers.

Granny Bumble, Honey, Mimosa and her mum and some of the other ballet girls and their mums all bundled through the door at once. Poppy knew she really was in trouble now.

Chapter Ten

"Poppy," began Granny Bumble, "Honey has been in such a state ever since you told her she had failed the exam—"

"So have Mimosa and all the other girls," said Mimosa's mum crossly, interrupting Granny Bumble.

"We just don't understand why you told Honey that everyone had failed the exam when it wasn't true," continued Granny Bumble, sounding disappointed rather than cross.

Each mum in turn had her say, telling
Poppy how much she had upset their
daughters and wanting to know why
she had told such a mean fib.

"When Sweetpea came home from the
shop crying and saying that she had seen
Honey and Mimosa and they'd told her
the bad news, I just couldn't believe it. It
was such a shock," said Sweetpea's mum.
"And after going to the city and spending
all that money on new ballet shoes."

"It certainly was a shock,"
agreed Natasha Melody.
"Abigail has never
failed an exam in
her life!"

Poppy
didn't know where
to look and was
grateful for Mum's
comforting arm

around her shoulders. She smiled
apologetically at Honey but Honey looked
away. *Oh no! It takes such a lot to make Honey
cross. This must be really bad!* she thought
miserably.

Poppy realized that she was going to have
to try to explain her mistake and she just
hoped that everyone would understand.

"Well, the thing is," she began, "when
Madame Angelwing was in the shop this
morning, I thought I heard her say to Mum
that everyone except me had failed the
ballet exam, so when I saw Honey and

Mimosa later on, I thought I should tell them even though it wasn't very good news."

"We saw Sweetpea in the shop just after that," explained Honey, "so we told her too."

"On my way home to tell my mum, I saw Abigail, so I told her about the results," added Sweetpea.

"And we all went to tell our mums," said the girls in chorus.

"I told my granny actually," said Honey.

"None of us could believe that they'd all failed," said the mums and Granny Bumble all together, "so we went to see Madame Angelwing, and that's where we bumped into each other and found out the truth!"

Poppy was waiting for everyone else to stop talking so that she could carry on with her explanation, and at last there was quiet.

"A bit later," she continued, "when I was talking to Miss Mallow and she told me that Madame Angelwing said that everyone had passed, I was really confused and I realized that I had mixed things up. I told Miss Mallow what had happened and then all of you arrived and started shouting," she explained in between small sobs. "I am really sorry. I didn't mean to upset anyone, especially not my friends."

Poppy's face was twisted with worry. How could she have set off such a chain of events? And how could all these usually lovely grown-ups be so cross?

"So—" resumed Granny Bumble, but just at that point a furious Madame Angelwing came striding through the door with a dramatic flourish.

"Poppy Cotton. Why have you fibbed about the ballet results? And why did you tell everyone in the village about my underwear – it is the talk of the Hedgerows Hotel and who knows where else!"

Poppy dissolved into more tears.

"Everyone! Just stop it for a moment, please," said Mum as she stroked Poppy's hair. "She's only a child. Anyway, it seems to me that it's not just Poppy who's been gossiping – everyone in the village has been doing it. If you remember, Madame, at first you said that you *thought* all these girls had failed. Poppy must have heard that and then repeated it to her friends, which she shouldn't have done. Before long, the story was all around the village, until it got back to the original source – you! I'm afraid I've got no idea where all this talk of underwear came from though," said Mum, stifling a giggle and looking directly at Poppy. "It certainly wasn't me!"

"Poppy knows she has made a mistake," added Miss Mallow. "She wasn't making the story up or telling fibs deliberately, she just heard it wrongly. It can happen to anyone. She knows that she shouldn't have been listening in the first place and that she certainly shouldn't have told anyone else what she heard – but admit it, we all gossip from time to time."

"Even so," butted in Granny Bumble, "Poppy should know better. Just look at all the trouble it's caused."

While all the mums and girls and Madame were chattering and bickering their way through the details of the mix-up, with everything getting more and more complicated every time someone added something new, a very cheerful and organized Saffron was walking the short

distance between Honeysuckle Cottage
and her shop.

"I'll just wave in the window," Saffron told
the twins, who cooed happily in agreement.
After a very wobbly start to the day she was
getting used to looking after Angel and
Archie. She wanted to show Aunt Lavender
and everyone else in the village how well she
was coping.

As Saffron got closer to the shop, she
spotted Poppy's fabulous new window
display.

"Oh, the princess theme is lovely!" she said to herself. "The little wardrobe looks just perfect. I've often thought it would look great but I've never had time to bring it upstairs. Wow, the shop is really busy!" she said to the twins. "I must get Aunt Lavender and Cousin Poppy to work here more often if they attract this many customers!"

As Saffron pushed open the door so that she could manoeuvre the pram inside, the sound of raised and squabbling voices

almost deafened her. The babies started to scream and Saffron began to panic. She had wanted everyone to see how happy the twins were in her care and how clean and tidy the big pram was too, but now she was feeling really out of control, and no one had noticed her come in because they were making so much noise themselves.

Eventually Mum caught sight of her. Then the others did too and they immediately fell into an embarrassed silence.

"What's going on here?" asked Saffron.

"I'm so sorry. There's been a bit of a mix-up and we're just trying to sort things out!" said Mum.

Chapter Eleven

While Mum explained everything to Saffron, with each mum and girl adding something to the whole sorry tale, as well as Madame Angelwing and Granny Bumble, Poppy sat on a little stool behind the counter with her hands over her ears. She wished she could start the whole day over again. The shouting and accusations had made her feel terrible; she decided to go for a walk to the Lavender Garden while Mum explained everything to Saffron. She couldn't bear to hear it all

again, so she slipped un-noticed out of the back door.

"Poppy just got a bit carried away with hearing so much gossip in here," Mum said. "I've already told her off today for her tall tales about you having problems with the twins when you were coping marvellously. I don't know why she says such things. Really, I don't," she finished, after summarizing the whole story.

"Well, actually, Poppy *was* sort of telling the truth about me not coping," said Saffron, and all the ladies in the shop quietened down so they could hear what she was saying. "She just exaggerated a little, that's all. We all do it, don't we? I even did it when you came back because I wanted you to think I was coping really well. The first part of the morning was just awful and I thought I would never manage. When Poppy came back, I was in a terrible state. And she very sweetly put on a puppet show for the twins while I had a break. If it hadn't been for her, I would never have got everything under control. And look at what she has done here. She has made a fabulous job of the window display. There's no need to be so hard on her."

As Saffron finished talking, a pretty young woman – the same one that Poppy and Mum had served that morning – came in. Her arrival was announced by the chiming of the bell. Mum made her way across the shop towards the woman, squeezing her way through all the upset girls and their irate mums.

"Hello, there. How nice to see you again. Have you decided to buy that dress for the wedding after all?" she asked, trying to prove to Saffron that she really had made a good job of looking after the shop.

"No, actually, I've got a confession to make," the woman replied, and everyone in the shop pricked up their ears, desperate to know what she was going to say next. "I'm not really going to a wedding at all. I'm Bryony Snow, a journalist from *Buttons and Bows* magazine, and I've been sent to the area to find the best clothes shop. And I've chosen this one because everything here is just stunning and beautifully made and the service I got this morning was the best I've ever had. The little girl who looked after me was so sweet and helpful. It's just a lovely family shop. So I'd like to give you this award. We'd also like to write an article on the business for next month's magazine *and* we've got two

free tickets to a fashion
show in New York next
season for you as part of
the prize," she concluded.

"That's wonderful news,"
smiled Mum, "but it's not actually my shop –
it belongs to my niece, Saffron."

So much for Charlie's gossip, thought Mum
as Saffron stepped forward, beaming with
pride.

"Wow! Thank you so much, Bryony. And
thank you, Aunt Lavender and Poppy, for
making such a good impression," said
Saffron, looking around the room for her
cousin. "Um, but where *is* Poppy? Has
anyone seen her?"

"Maybe she's in the workshop?" suggested
Madame Angelwing with concern. "Mimosa,
be a darling and go and have a look."

But there was a deafening silence in the
basement.

"We must go and look for her right away!" said Madame Angelwing. "We've been too harsh with her – she's only a girl. What does it matter if she has been gossiping a little and everybody knows about my big knickers? We all do it, don't we, ladies?"

Chapter Thirteen

Mum put on her sensible shoes and made
her way towards the village, with Granny
Bumble and Honey following close behind.
Saffron came too, pushing the pram and
trying to keep the twins entertained, and
behind her were all Poppy's ballet friends
and their mums, as well as Bryony Snow,
bringing up the rear of a huge Honeypot
Hill conga.

First they checked Poppy's tree house. But
there was no one there.

Then they tried Grandpa's house, but he
hadn't seen her. Next they went to the
adventure playground, but she wasn't there
either.

"This is hopeless," said Mum, feeling
absolutely desperate. "Where is she?"

"I've got an idea, Mrs Cotton," said Honey
quietly. "Follow me."

Finally they found Poppy sitting alone in
the Lavender Garden.

"Thank goodness!" everyone gasped.

Mum ran over to hug her. "Darling, we've
been so worried. Why did you run off?"

"Because I caused so much trouble and

everyone is so cross with me for gossiping
and I didn't think anyone liked me any
more," said Poppy. "I really didn't mean to
upset anyone – I was just trying to be
helpful and pass on news and I think I got
a bit carried away. I wish today had never
happened."

Everyone gathered round her to give
her a hug.

"Of course we still like you, sweetheart,"
said Granny Bumble kindly. "In fact, we've
realized that we've all been a bit too hard on

you. We know that you didn't set out to cause trouble or upset anyone, but I hope you've learned your lesson. Let's just forget it now."

"Thanks, Granny Bumble. I am truly sorry, all of you. I promise I won't gossip again, even if it's as funny as Madame Angelwing's bloomers!" replied Poppy cheekily, and everyone laughed, even the ballet teacher.

"I know what!" said Granny Bumble cheerfully. "Let's play Chinese Whispers and see if we can all stick to the right story!"

"Great!" cried the girls. They loved this game.

The girls stood in a line and Granny Bumble took some paper and a pen out of her handbag and wrote down a whisper message. She thought very carefully

Princess Poppy is certainly a princess after all!

about what to write until she came up with
something that she thought would be perfect.
She wrote: *Princess Poppy is certainly a princess
after all.* The message was whispered from
Poppy to Honey. When Honey turned to
Mimosa, Mimosa heard: *Princess Poppy is
certainly going to be a princess after all.* And
when Mimosa turned to Abigail, Abigail
heard: *Princess Poppy is certainly going to a
princess ball.* Sweetpea was the last to hear
the message and had to say it out loud to
all the others. The message she heard was:

Princess Poppy is going to be the belle of a princess ball.

Granny Bumble laughed and told the girls what the message had actually been. Everyone understood just what she meant – and also that not another word would be said on the matter.

Gradually all the mums and girls left the Lavender Garden and Mum, Poppy, Saffron and the twins and Bryony Snow were the only people left.

"I am so sorry," said Poppy.

"Just forget all about it, sweetheart. The rest of us have been doing our fair share of gossiping too!" said Saffron. "You're still our princess – so long as you don't gossip again, especially not about me!"

Poppy hugged her cousin, and it was only then that she noticed Bryony Snow standing next to the pram.

Mum saw Poppy's bemused expression and smiled. "Oh, of course, you haven't met Bryony Snow properly," she said as she introduced the journalist to Poppy and explained all about the award and the amazing prize.

"Wow! That's so brilliant," said Poppy, beaming with pride and desperately hoping Saffron would take her to New York with her next season. She *had* actually managed to do something good that day after all!

"Poppy, it's so nice to meet you again," smiled Bryony. "You played a huge part in

my decision to choose Saffron's Sewing Shop
as the winner because you were so sweet and
helpful this morning. Thank you! I am
definitely going to mention you, and your
cousin and mum, in my article about the
shop for next month's magazine. Speaking of
that, I really must get back to the office and
do some work on it," explained Bryony, then
she waved goodbye and walked off in the
direction of Honeypot Hill station.

"Wasn't it funny how Granny's message got changed and how I got it so wrong about the thief?" she commented as they walked back to the shop.

"Yes, it just shows how easily things can get mixed up!" agreed Mum.

"I wish I *was* going to a princess ball!" said Poppy wistfully.

"Well, the village party could be a sort of princess ball. The only problem is, what will you wear?" laughed Mum.

"I've got the perfect dress for Poppy in my workshop," said Saffron. "I've been keeping it a secret for her. In fact I was going to give it to you as a thank you for working in the shop. Just wait until you see it, Poppy. It was inspired by the lilac tree in Grandpa's garden."

"Yippee!" cried Poppy. She didn't like to say that she had already spied that dress! And even danced around the workshop with it!

When Mum and Poppy finally got home
with the babies, Mum fed them and put
them to bed. Then they sat down to supper –
beautifully prepared by Saffron.

"How was your day?" asked Dad, eager
to hear all the news from the shop.

"Fine," said Mum and Poppy. They didn't
want to gossip any more.

THE END

*Turn over to read an extract from
the next Princess Poppy book,*
The Haunted Holiday . . .

Chapter One

"Bonjour, Honey!" called Poppy as her best friend arrived with her suitcase and backpack. "All ready for the holiday?"

"Bonjour to you too!" called Honey. "I've been packed for days – I'm so excited. How've the French lessons with your grandpa been going?"

"Très bien!" said Poppy, showing off. "But learning all the vocabulary is really difficult and a bit boring. I love hearing all about French history though. Grandpa makes

it sound so interesting – he's been telling me about the French Revolution. The last Queen of France was Marie Antoinette. She had hair as high as a top hat and she wore dresses as fancy as a wedding dress every day! Grandpa told me that the French people decided that they didn't want to have kings and queens and princes and princesses any more so they just got rid of them. That's what the French Revolution was."

"Gosh, but why would anyone *not* want real princesses?" said Honey. "They must have been mad!"

Poppy shrugged her shoulders. She couldn't understand it either. "Who knows? It's such a terrible waste of beautiful palaces and tiaras and stuff," she said sadly.

"Exactly," agreed Honey.

"And guess what else Grandpa told me," said Poppy. "It's really gross!"

"What?" asked Honey, fascinated.

"People had their heads cut off by the revolutionaries!"

"I don't believe it. That's too cruel." Honey shuddered; she found it hard to imagine that such a thing could ever have happened. "I just can't wait to see my mum and dad again when we get to France," she said, deliberately changing the subject because she didn't want to hear any more about people having their heads chopped off. "It's been ages since I last saw them."

Poppy had always thought it strange that
Honey didn't live with her parents all the
time, but Honey had often explained that
her mum and dad had to travel a lot for
work. Honey's dad was a film producer and
her mum was a successful actress. After they
got married and had Honey, they had
planned to settle down in Honeypot Hill.
However, they needed to keep jetting about
the world for their work, so it was agreed
that Granny Bumble would keep Honey safe

at home. That way Honey was able to go to school and make friends there. Granny Bumble was a wonderful full-time parent, but that didn't stop Honey wishing that her mum and dad were around all the time.

Just then they heard the toot of a horn. It was Poppy's cousin Saffron and her husband David, the village vet. They were accompanying the girls on the flight: Saffron was off to the Paris fashion shows to get some inspiration for her new collection and David was going with her. Meanwhile Poppy and Honey were going to stay with Honey's parents in the historic Chateau de Lafayette, which they had rented for the whole summer. Daniel Bumble, Honey's dad, was working on new film ideas and thought that a couple of months in a French castle might inspire him! Saffron and David were going to join the girls at Chateau de Lafayette in the middle of the week, and

Poppy's family and Granny Bumble were
flying over a couple of days later for a long
weekend as Granny Bumble's birthday treat.

The girls climbed into David's car and
waved goodbye to Mum, Dad, the twins,
Grandpa and Granny Bumble.

"I can't wait to see Chateau de Lafayette,"
said Saffron on the way to the airport. "I just
love the atmosphere in old buildings. What's
it like, Honey?"

"Well, I haven't actually been there before,
but Mum and Dad told me that it's hundreds
of years old and really, really big, and it has
a really interesting history. I hope nothing

too horrible happened there though!" said
Honey, remembering what Poppy had told
her earlier. "It used to belong to a French
noble family called the de Lafayettes," she
continued, "and my mum says it looks like a
giant fairy castle."

"Maybe it's haunted," said David, making
a spooky woooo-woooo noise.

"David, just concentrate on the driving!"
said Saffron.

"Just teasing," he smiled. "Actually, I wish I
was coming straight to the castle instead of
being dragged round the fashion shows. It'll
be so much more fun than admiring

stick-insect models in boring black outfits all day long."

Even though she knew David had been teasing them, Poppy couldn't get what he had said out of her mind – what if the castle *was* haunted? It would be so exciting.